Bats in the Air, Bats in My Hair

Written By: Martha Hamlett
Illustrated By: Davey Morgan

AuthorHouse™
1663 Liberty Drive
Bloomington, IN 47403
www.authorhouse.com
Phone: 833-262-8899

Because of the dynamic nature of the Internet, any web addresses or links contained in this book may have changed since publication and may no longer be valid. The views expressed in this work are solely those of the author and do not necessarily reflect the views of the publisher, and the publisher hereby disclaims any responsibility for them.

Any people depicted in stock imagery provided by Getty Images are models, and such images are being used for illustrative purposes only.
Certain stock imagery © Getty Images.

This book is printed on acid-free paper.

ISBN: 978-1-4389-2358-1 (sc)
ISBN: 978-1-4634-5600-9 (e)

Print information available on the last page.

Published by AuthorHouse 10/13/2020

authorHOUSE

Bats in the Air, Bats in my Hair

Martha Hamlett
Author

Dedicated to my three special guys - Phillip, Noah and Christian.

Davey Morgan
Illustrator

Dedicated to my dazzling Marissa.

To Grandmother's house Sally did go.
How long she would stay, she did not know.

She arrived at eight and went straight to bed. On Grandmother's pillow she rested her head.

She closed her eyes and fell asleep.
From her room, no one heard a peep.

Then about midnight she awoke with a strange feeling, That something was moving about in the ceiling.

She heard a squeak,
then a flutter.
She jumped out of bed
with a shudder.

They wiggled on the floor,
As she ran for the door.

They flew into the hall.
Some smashed into the wall.

She picked up a broom and swung at the creatures, But baseball had never been one of her star features.

So as fast as she could
she ran from the room.
She never even bothered
to put down the broom.

She ran to her Grandmother without looking back.
She tried to explain she was under attack.

"BATS, BATS," was all she could say,
As her Grandmother took the broom away.

Shhh!

Down the hall they both walked
quiet as a mouse.
They hoped their visitors
were no longer in the house.

But to their dismay
when they turned on the light,
Those creepy, little creatures
began to take flight.

click

"Open the window," her Grandmother cried.
Sally couldn't budge it no matter how hard she tried.

They tugged and pulled on the window together.
They just had to get rid of those bats forever.

The window flew open,
and Grandmother grabbed the broom.
She swept those bats
right out of the room.

They closed the window and latched it tight.
There was only one more thing to do that night.

Grandmother grabbed some rags and tape,
And fixed the place of the great escape.

Sally was relieved and quite elated,
Now that those bats had been evacuated.

She crawled into bed
and fell into a slumber,
But she dreamed of those bats
in great number.

They were in the air and in her hair.
All through the night they were everywhere.

The next morning, home she did go.
When she would come back, she did not know.

Printed in the United States
By Bookmasters